To Maegan ~
Best Wishes
Susan Jane Ryan
2008

Esmeralda
and the
Enchanted Pond

Written by

Susan Jane Ryan

Illustrated by

Sandra G. Cook

🍍 PINEAPPLE PRESS, INC. SARASOTA, FLORIDA

Inquiries should be addressed to:

Pineapple Press, Inc.
P.O. Box 3889
Sarasota, Florida 34230

www.pineapplepress.com

Library of Congress Cataloging-in-Publication Data

Ryan, Susan Jane.
Esmeralda and the enchanted pond / Susan Jane Ryan ; illustrations by Sandra Cook.—1st ed.
p.   cm.
Summary: Esmeralda learns some simple science lessons as well as lessons in using her imagination when she and her dad visit a pond during all four seasons and see a variety of forest creatures.
ISBN 1-56164-236-3
[1. Ponds—Fiction. 2. Nature study—Fiction. 3. Seasons—Fiction. 4. Imagination—Fiction.
5. Fathers and daughters—Fiction.] I. Cook, Sandra, 1954– ill.

PZ7.R9575 Es 2001
[E]—dc21
2001021364

First Edition
10 9 8 7 6 5 4 3 2 1

DESIGN BY CAROL TORNATORE CREATIVE DESIGN

Printed in China

*E*smeralda Guinevere Smith loved to go to the pond with her father. Each Saturday, she and her dad would drive to the forest and walk down the shaded path to their secret place. Her dad carried a backpack, and inside were a blanket, sandwiches, cold drinks, and gooey chocolate cake. Sometimes they would bring books to read.

The path meandered through the shady, cool woods. Then, without warning, Esmeralda and her dad would come out to a sunny area and see the whole pond at one time. Cypress trees surrounded one side, and tall stalks of grass and lily pads with yellow flowers floated in the water. If Esmeralda and her dad were very quiet, they would usually see a great blue heron wading in the water and several turtles sunning themselves on fallen logs.

*E*smeralda's dad liked to call this part of the forest the "Enchanted Fairy Pond." He would tell Esmeralda that if she looked quickly out of the sides of her eyes she would see fairies dancing on the petals of the black-eyed Susans. Esmeralda would get mad, scrunch up her face and say, "They're dragonflies, Daddy. You know that!"

"Shh, Esmeralda. You'll wake the sleeping gnomes," he would say and point to the sunning turtles.

"Turtles, Dad. They're just turtles." Esmeralda would then shrug her shoulders, give up, and wish that her parents had just named her Jane or Mary.

*T*oday, Esmeralda and her dad silently walked down the moss-covered path. She could smell the pine trees in the fresh spring air. The early morning sunlight was just streaming through the leafy branches. As they rounded the corner, they saw an amazing sight. The mist from the pond was rising mysteriously into the air. A swallow-tailed kite was swooping over the water clutching a small snake in its claws. The bird flew higher in the air and landed on a branch of a dead cypress tree. There it had its breakfast.

"Wow," whispered Esmeralda.

"Wow," said her dad. "An amazing sight!"

Esmeralda looked at her dad with a quizzical expression and asked, "Dad, what makes the mist rise from the pond?"

Esmeralda's dad looked at her with a serious expression, leaned toward her and said, "The evil king from the land of Blarney put a spell on the Enchanted Fairy Pond. What you see is the mist of magic holding the spell in place."

"C'mon, Dad. Tell me for real. I want to know," Esmeralda pleaded.

"OK, Esmeralda. If you really must know . . . ," said her dad, the twinkle in his eye slowly fading. "The water is warmer than the air in the morning. So the water evaporates into the air into something invisible called water vapor. Then the water vapor hits the colder air above the pond and condenses into little droplets on the dust that is

floating in the air. That is what you call mist. As
the sun warms the air, the mist evaporates and the
water vapor rises into the sky."

"Thanks, Dad," said Esmeralda, satisfied with her dad's answer.

For the rest of the morning, Esmeralda and her dad went exploring. They found bright blue pickerel weed just beginning to bloom around the edges of the pond. They heard a cricket frog's *click click* interrupting the quiet of the morning. They watched a blue-tailed skink scurry on a log chasing small insects. The fresh spring air made them hungry for lunch. After they ate, they both relaxed on the blanket and read their books. Soon it was time to go home.

As the summer days lengthened and the heat of the forest rose in the thick, bug-filled air, Esmeralda and her dad walked down the lush, green path to their Enchanted Fairy Pond once again. A mockingbird trilled their arrival as they rounded the bend and approached the water. The noonday sun created a blinding glare off the water. Esmeralda could see two eyes sticking up from the deep, dark pool. The creature remained motionless as Esmeralda grabbed her dad's arm.

"Look, Dad," she whispered.

"Ah, how lucky we are. It's the fairy queen of the pond herself, here to greet us. Too bad she is still under the magic spell of the evil king from the land of Blarney," her dad said with a twinkle in his eye.

"Gator, Dad," exclaimed Esmeralda. "It's just an old alligator."

The gator quietly slid under the water and glided to the other side of the pond.

"I think you offended the queen, Esmeralda," her dad explained. "That's why she left."

"Oh, Dad!" exclaimed Esmeralda in disgust.

"C'mon, Esmeralda. Let's see what we can find," said her dad.

The two walked slowly around the pond looking for amazing sights. They saw bees swarming around the soft, yellow, pincushion-like buttonbush blooms. They watched a woodpecker dig for insects in a sweet gum tree.

"Look, Esmeralda." Her dad pointed to a cluster of pink flowers close to the ground. "These are pink sundews. They eat meat. They're carnivorous."

"Sure, Dad. Is this another one of your stories?"

"No, Esmeralda, this is for real. Insects are attracted to the sticky substance on the leaves and get caught. Then the plant uses them for food."

"Ugh!" said Esmeralda.

*E*smeralda and her dad spread out their blanket in the clearing by the pond and ate their lunch. After they had eaten their fill, Esmeralda lay back on the blanket and looked up. She watched the clouds billow and rise in the afternoon sky. As time passed, the clouds turned dark and ominous.

She turned to her dad and asked, "What makes those clouds form, Dad?"

"Clouds?" he replied. "What clouds, Esmeralda? Those are not clouds at all. Those are the sheep of the fairies. The evil king from the land of Blarney has put them in the sky so no one can free them. Every afternoon, he shears the wool and piles it high." He grinned at Esmeralda, hoping she would play along.

"Please, Dad. Give me a break. I want to know about clouds, not fairy sheep," she exclaimed loudly as she scrunched up her face in anger.

"OK, Esmeralda. If you really want to know . . . ," said her dad. "Water vapor evaporates from ponds, lakes, rivers, and oceans and rises up into the sky. Higher up, the air temperature cools down and the water vapor condenses on little dust particles, forming the white, puffy clouds you see. The water droplets in the clouds combine, get heavy, and fall as rain."

*J*ust as Esmeralda's dad finished his explanation, a giant raindrop plopped right onto Esmeralda's head. The two of them quickly gathered their things together, stuffed them into the backpack, and hurried back down the trail. A deep roll of thunder sounded in the air.

Esmeralda's dad grinned at her and said, "Ah, the evil king from the land of Blarney is telling us to go home."

"Oh, Dad, really!" exclaimed Esmeralda.

$\mathcal{I}$t was a cool October day when Esmeralda and her dad walked down the path toward the Enchanted Fairy Pond. Leaves crunched underfoot. A huge banana spider sat, patiently waiting for unsuspecting insects. Small drops of moisture glistened on the spokes of the spider's web, making it appear to be made of woven silver threads.

"Ah, it's the enchanted fairy prince guarding the entrance to the pond, Esmeralda," said her dad.

"Spider, Dad," she exclaimed indignantly. "Big, yellow spider!"

Esmeralda's dad grinned and said, "I think you're mistaken. The evil king from the land of Blarney cast a spell on the fairy prince. He has to be a spider for two hundred thirty-seven days. I think he has just thirty-four days left."

"Dad, you're impossible," Esmeralda exclaimed as she put both hands on her hips and shook her head in disbelief.

$\mathcal{E}$smeralda and her dad rounded the bend, and there before them was the Enchanted Fairy Pond. A large fox squirrel was sitting on a branch of a cypress tree on the other side of the pond. It was grayish black with a long, bushy tail. In its paws it clutched a seed. The squirrel looked up at the two of them, decided he was safe and continued eating.

"Wow!" said Esmeralda.

"Amazing!" said her dad.

The two of them walked slowly around the pond. The cypress needles were turning brown and falling off the trees. Some late-blooming arrowhead bordered the pond, their white blossoms and arrow-shaped leaves providing some fall decoration.

Esmeralda walked up to the edge of the water and tried to see the bottom. The water was a dark tea color. Bits of cypress needles and other plant debris floated on the surface.

"Dad, why is the water this brown color? Is it polluted?"

"No, Esmeralda, not polluted. Just enchanted. When the evil king from the land of Blarney put a spell on this pond, he declared that the water should remain dark, just like his magic spell." Esmeralda's dad looked at her sideways with his eyebrows raised and a small smile pulling at the corners of his mouth.

"Puh-leeze, Dad. I asked you a real question. I want a real answer." Esmeralda stamped her foot in frustration.

"OK, Esmeralda, if that's what you really want." Her father's face took on a serious expression as he began his explanation. "This pond is surrounded by cypress trees. These trees and other plants in the wetlands have a chemical in them called tannic acid. When it rains, the water flushes this tannic acid into the pond, causing the tea color you see."

"Thanks, Dad. How am I going to learn if you don't tell me?" Esmeralda felt very wise indeed.

*E*smeralda looked down at the shoreline and noticed several different sets of animal tracks embedded in the sand.

"Look at this, Dad." She pointed to the tracks. "I think these were made by a deer."

"You're absolutely right, Esmeralda," he said as he recognized the split-hoofed markings. "And these were made by a raccoon." In the sand were little five-fingered paw prints.

"This must be the place the animals come in the morning to get a drink, Esmeralda. The next time we come, let's get here very early and maybe we can see something really special."

*E*smeralda and her dad walked down the pathway toward the Enchanted Fairy Pond. It was very early in the morning and very cold. The Spanish moss swayed in the icy January breeze. They passed a water oak. Esmeralda looked up and saw a patch of bright green in the middle of the bare branches.

"What's that, Dad?" she asked, pointing up.

"Why, Esmeralda, that's the only part of the forest the evil king from the land of Blarney did not cast a spell on."

"Dad," said Esmeralda, giving her father a warning look.

"No, really. Look around you. The trees are bare. The flowers are gone. Only that one plant reminds us that spring will come soon," replied her dad with a twinkle in his eye.

"Really, Dad, what is that plant?" she demanded.

"OK, Esmeralda. If you really must know, that's a parasite called mistletoe. It stays green all year 'round. It's an evergreen."

"Is that what you hang over the doorway in the kitchen at Christmas so you can kiss Mom when she comes in?"

"The very same, Esmeralda. See, there is magic in that plant!"

"Oh, Dad," said Esmeralda with exasperation.

The two of them silently walked down the path together. As they neared the bend, Esmeralda's dad motioned for her to be very, very quiet. They tiptoed the last few remaining yards to the pond. As they neared it, they saw a most amazing sight. At the water's edge was a beautiful, soft brown doe. Her head was bent down towards the water and she was drinking. The two of them stood motionless and just watched. Soon she had her fill and disappeared gracefully into the woods.

"Wow!" said Esmeralda's dad, clutching her arm.

"Wow!" said Esmeralda. "That was incredible."

"Yes, I can't believe we saw the beautiful fairy princess herself!"

Esmeralda looked at her dad in utter disbelief. "Deer, Dad. A big, brown deer. Haven't you figured it out yet? I'm too old for pretending."

"Who's pretending?" said her dad, shrugging his shoulders with his hands outstretched.

*E*smeralda shivered as the wind picked up. She looked at the pond, which was usually still and peaceful. The surface was rippled and wavy. Little patches of foam collected near the shore around the cypress knees. A red-tailed hawk was perched high in the dead cypress tree, its feathers ruffling in the wind.

"What's happening to our peaceful pond, Dad?" she asked with concern in her voice.

"Well, Esmeralda, if you look high in that cypress tree, you'll see the evil king from the land of Blarney disguised as a hawk. He is angry today and has asked the wind ogre to blow and bluster."

"Dad, I'm not kidding. Just answer the question," she pleaded.

"OK, Esmeralda. If you must know, the wind is blowing over the water, causing the waves, ripples, and bubbles. Even though it looks pretty rough out there, it's really a good thing. The wind action is adding oxygen to the water for the plants, fish, and other animals that live under the water."

"Thanks, Dad," said Esmeralda. "I appreciate your honest answer."

Esmeralda's dad shivered in the cold wind. He looked a little sad. He took hold of Esmeralda's hand and said, "Come on, Esmeralda, let's go home. We'll come back when it's warmer."

$\mathcal{I}$t had been several months since Esmeralda and her dad had visited the Enchanted Fairy Pond. Esmeralda was excited as they walked down the path in the early morning sun. The leaves on the trees had just come out, and the forest was awash with every color green imaginable. An anole scurried up the trunk of a pine tree as they passed by. A marsh rabbit darted across the path.

"Hurry, Dad. I can't wait to get there," said Esmeralda impatiently.

"Slow down, Esmeralda. We don't want to scare the animals away," he replied.

The two of them reached the bend and tiptoed down the path. There before them was a most amazing sight! The doe they had seen during the winter was drinking at the pond, and with her was a spotted, spindly-legged fawn!

Esmeralda gasped in amazement. The doe lifted her head, listened intently, and bounded off into the forest with her fawn trailing quickly behind her.

"Wow!" said Esmeralda.

"Wow!" said her dad. "The doe had a baby fawn."

Esmeralda stopped and looked at her dad in disbelief. She thought for a moment and spoke.

"Dad, I think you're mistaken. That wasn't a doe at all. That was the fairy princess. With her is

her newborn child, who will one day be king of
the fairies. He will challenge the evil king from the
land of Blarney to a duel and win!"

*E*smeralda's dad looked at her with a twinkle in his eye, lifted her off the ground, swung her around in a circle, and exclaimed, "Esmeralda, you are absolutely right!"

If you enjoyed reading this book, here are some other books from Pineapple Press on related topics. For a complete catalog, write to Pineapple Press, P.O. Box 3889, Sarasota, FL 34230 or call 1-800-PINEAPL (746-3275). Or visit our website at www.pineapplepress.com.

Drawing Florida Wildlife by Frank Lohan. Whether you want to learn a new skill or improve your drawing skills, the easy directions in this guide will help you. Contains the clearest, easiest method yet for learning to draw birds, reptiles, amphibians, and mammals. Each section includes a partially finished drawing for you to complete. ISBN 1-56164-090-5 (pb)

The Florida Water Story by Peggy Sias Lantz and Wendy A. Hale. Illustrates and describes many of the plants and animals that depend on the springs, rivers, beaches, marshes, and reefs in and around Florida, including corals, sharks, lobsters, alligators, manatees, birds, turtles, and fish. Suggests ways everyone can help protect Florida's priceless natural resources. ISBN 1-56164-099-9 (hb)

Florida's Fossils by Robin Brown. Includes a complete identification section and insightful comments on the history of the fossil treasures you'll uncover. Budding archaeologists will appreciate updated maps and directions to some of the best fossil-hunting areas in Florida. ISBN 1-56164-114-6 (pb)

Legends of the Seminoles by Betty Mae Jumper. Illustrated in color, this book contains Seminole legends that have never existed in print before. Listen to stories that introduce adventurers, human and animal, and explain why the world is the way it is. For readers and listeners of all ages. ISBN 1-56164-033-6 (hb); ISBN 1-56164-040-9 (pb)

The Young Naturalist's Guide to Florida by Peggy Sias Lantz and Wendy A. Hale. Plants, birds, insects, reptiles, and mammals are all around us. Complete with a glossary, this enticing book shows you where to look for Florida's most interesting natural features and creatures. Take it along on your next walk in the woods! ISBN 1-56164-051-4 (pb)